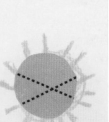
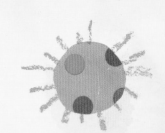

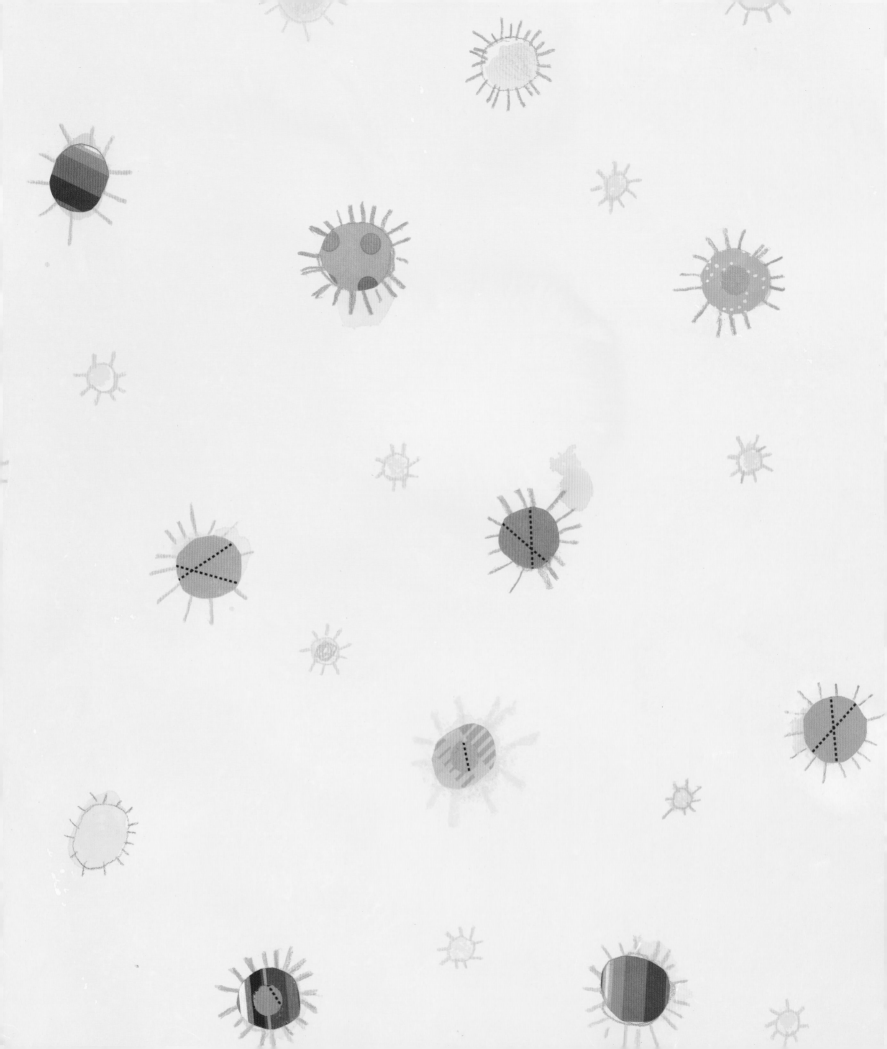

BABY BEAR'S BIG DREAMS

illustrated by
MELISSA SWEET

written by
JANE YOLEN

HARCOURT, INC.

Orlando Austin New York San Diego Toronto London

Requests for permission to make copies of any
part of the work should be submitted online at
www.harcourt.com/contact or mailed to the
following address: Permissions Department,
Harcourt, Inc., 6277 Sea Harbor Drive,
Orlando, Florida 32887-6777.

www.HarcourtBooks.com

Library of Congress Cataloging-in-Publication Data
Yolen, Jane.
Baby Bear's big dreams/written by Jane Yolen; illustrated by Melissa Sweet.
p. cm.
Summary: A baby bear dreams of all the wonderful things he will be able to do when
he is grown, from staying up late to building a house in a honey tree.
[1. Growth—Fiction. 2. Bears—Fiction. 3. Stories in rhyme.] I. Sweet, Melissa, ill. II. Title.
PZ8.3.Y76Bac 2007
[E]—dc22   2006009247
ISBN 978-0-15-205291-1

First edition
A B C D E F G H

Manufactured in China

The illustrations in this book were done in mixed media and collage on watercolor paper.
The display and text type were set in Kosmik.
Color separations by Bright Arts Ltd., Hong Kong
Manufactured by South China Printing Company, Ltd., China
Production supervision by Christine Witnik
Designed by Linda Lockowitz and Scott Piehl

For Liz Van Doren, who helps her authors dream big
—J. Y.

For Charles and Victoria
—M. S.

When I grow up
in about a year,
my special friends
will move in here.

We'll play all day
and stay up late,
and never go to bed
by eight.

The toys will not
be put away
but left around
for play next day.

In fact, play never
will be through,
for that's what
big bears always do.

When I grow up
in a year or two,
I know just what
I'm going to do.

I'll live in a shop
that's filled with toys—
a few for girls
and LOTS for boys...

with carousels
for taking rides
and puffer trains
and giant slides.

I'll paint pictures
red and blue,
for that's what
big bears always do.

When I grow up
in a year or three,
I'll build a house
in a honey tree.

And when it's time
for me to eat,
I'll pick some berries
at my feet.

My friends will come
around for tea
and honey cakes
up in my tree.

They'll stay and play
a week or two,
for that's what
big bears always do.

air mail

When I grow up
in a year or four,
I'll get a tent
and go explore.

I'll wear brown boots
and a feathered hat,
and bring along
a sleeping mat.

I'll climb high up
a big fir tree—
paw after paw,
most carefully.

I'll look around,
admire the view,
for that's what
big bears always do.

When I grow up
in a year or five,
I'll take some honey
from a hive,
and tie it
with a bright red bow,
and visit other bears
I know.

Then by ourselves,
we'll play some cards,
and after, race
around their yards
in games of tag
and peekaboo,
for that's what
big bears always do.

When I'm ALL grown,
I'll come back home
and read aloud
my growing poem.

Mama and Papa
will say, "Well done,"
and give bear hugs
to their grown-up son,

then tuck me in
my special bed,
with giant pillows
for my head,
and give me kisses,
one and two . . .

for that's what
BIG bears always do.